D1215096

Virginia
and the
Tiny One

Books by Esther Bender

Lemon Tree Series
Katie and the Lemon Tree
Virginia and the Tiny One

Picture Storybooks
April Bluebird
The Crooked Tree
Search for a Fawn

Mystery
Shadow at Sun Lake

Meditations
A Cry from the Clay

Study Guide for The Crooked Tree

Book Orders: 1-800-759-4447
Study Guide Orders: PO Box 732,
Grantsville, MD 21536

Virginia
and the
Tiny One

Esther Bender

Illustrated by Joy Dunn Keenan

Herald
Press

Scottdale, Pennsylvania
Waterloo, Ontario

Library of Congress Cataloging-in-Publication Data

Bender, Esther, 1942–
    Virginia and the tiny one / Esther Bender : illustrated
by Joy Dunn Keenan.
        p. cm. — (Lemon tree series)
    Sequel to: Katie and the lemon tree.
    Summary: While living with her family in a remote
mountain area of western Maryland during the 1850s,
thirteen-year-old Virginia, granddaughter of German
immigrants, learns to grow in faith.
    ISBN 0-8361-9090-4 (alk. paper)
    [1. Frontier and pioneer life—Fiction. 2. German
Americans—Fiction. 3. Christian life—Fiction. 4. Family
life—Fiction.]
    I. Keenan, Joy Dunn, 1952- ill. II. Title. III. Series:
Bender, Esther. 1942- Lemon tree series.
PZ7.B4313Vi   1998
[Fic]--dc21   98-20317
                                                      AC

The paper used in this publication is recycled and meets
the minimum requirements of the American National
Standard for Information Sciences—Permanence of Paper
for Printed Library Materials, ANSI Z39.48-1984.

VIRGINIA AND THE TINY ONE
Copyright © 1998 by Herald Press, Scottdale, Pa. 15683
    Published simultaneously in Canada by Herald Press,
    Waterloo, Ont. N2L 6H7. All rights reserved
Library of Congress Catalog Card Number: 98-20317
International Standard Book Number: 0-8361-9090-4
Printed in the United States of America
Cover art by Joy Dunn Keenan
Book design by Jim Butti

07 06 05 04 03 02 01 00 99 98 10 9 8 7 6 5 4 3 2 1

To Ernest and Amelia Brenneman,
parents of triplets,
and the two who lived,
Alvin and Allen

Contents

Living the Promises!
The Dreams!

Katie and the Lemon Tree tells how Katie Miller came to America in the early 1800s with her young husband, Daniel. They were Anabaptist immigrants from Germany. Anabaptists did not baptize babies. Instead, they baptized persons old enough and willing to claim the Christian faith for themselves.

Katie came to America for the promises of religious freedom and low-cost land. She found room for dreams.

The promises of America pulled her onward. Katie left Germany forever. She left her family forever. She took a long and dangerous voyage. She learned to live in a strange land. Katie did it all so her children would not have to live in fear that their lives were in danger because of what they believed.

In Germany, the years of capture, torture, and death for Anabaptists were over. Yet stories of what had happened to their ancestors lingered like spiders in the hair. *Would they bite again?*

The Anabaptists were not popular. They kept to their own congregations rather than meeting with churches favored by the princes. They did not want to take part in the wars of Europe. The promise of America was freedom from fear and unfair treatment.

In Germany, Katie and Daniel knew they could never buy a farm. Rich noblemen owned the land. In America, there was still unclaimed space. Land was cheap. America promised free or low-cost land.

The fictional but true-to-life Millers arrived in Baltimore. They traveled west into the Allegheny mountains. On a high plateau, they found inexpensive land. There they settled and raised a family. So the promises were fulfilled.

What of the dreams? Katie dreamed of sending money to Germany for her parents to come to America. She dreamed of finding friends and a church community. She dreamed of a prosperous homestead.

These dreams were fulfilled by "keeping the faith and milking the cow." This is a proverb made up by Katie's mother. It means to keep working toward something, even when it seems impossible. The dreams were fulfilled. This story is told in *Katie and the Lemon Tree.*

• • •

Now in this sequel, *Virginia and the Tiny One*, Katie is Grandma Katie to Virginia, age thirteen. Virginia has never known fear of religious persecution. Virginia's father, Daniel, owns land, and her grandfather Daniel owns land. Persecution and owning land are not concerns of Virginia. Her generation lives out her grandmother's promises and dreams without those worries.

This story about Virginia shows the family's life

10

in the late 1850s. Virginia has to help care for younger children *and* do housework. She goes to school, but only through grade 8. In her time, most states don't have laws to send all children to school. Many girls do not attend at all or drop out before finishing grade 8.

Religious influence is still strong in Virginia's family. They remain loyal to their Christian beliefs.

In this remote mountain area, Virginia grows up with dreams of winning a spelling bee. She expects that someday she will marry and have children. Many other girls are marrying in their late teens.

However, Virginia first must do what seems impossible. She suddenly has a job she doesn't know how to do. Life depends on her. She has little chance of success. Will she give up?

Like her grandmother, she sails across an unknown ocean. Sail with her as she learns to act in faith!

1

In the Night

Listen! He is whistling in the night.
Listen! She is singing in the night
"Away in a manger, no crib for a bed,
The little Lord Jesus laid down his sweet head."
From time long past
comes the echo of their song,
the song of faith.

Upstairs, in the middle of the night—Christmas Eve—Virginia began to awake when Papa shook her shoulder. "Ginny and Sarah, wake up! Put on your shoes."

She felt his fingers. His voice was still far away. He shook her again! His words became a loud command: "Virginia, wake up!"

Virginia Miller blinked. The lantern swung in front of her eyes, blinding her. Papa's face, with his dark beard, was a blur behind the lantern. He set it down and pulled her arms so she had to sit up. "Get up, now! Ginny! You have to get up now!"

"Why? What's happening?" she asked.

Papa didn't answer. He said, "Put on your stockings and shoes. Never mind putting on a dress. Just leave your nightgown on."

Virginia threw back the heavy quilts that covered her, then swung her long legs out of bed. She shivered when her feet touched the ice-cold wooden floor. Quickly she began pulling on her stockings and shoes. The ruffle of her long white nightgown got in her way, but she yanked it up impatiently.

Her blonde hair, which had been braided the day before, rippled nearly to her waist. At thirteen, everyone said she looked just like her mother, Christina. When her mother was eighteen, she had married Daniel Miller. Two years later, Daniel III had been born, then the next year Virginia, and seven years later, Sarah.

Now Virginia saw with surprise that her brother, Danny, was sitting in a chair by the bed. He was already dressed, but his head nodded sleepily. Had he, too, been awakened and told to get dressed on such a cold winter night? Why?

Papa shook little Sarah's shoulders again and sat her up. He put on her shoes. Her head nodded as she fell asleep again. Sarah's baby-fine straight hair made a soft halo around her head.

"Come on, Danny." Papa shook him.

Danny's head was down. He was the only one with Papa's hair, dark and wavy. Now his head lifted as he awoke again. Virginia's nose wrinkled as she smelled his barn clothes.

Papa led Sarah downstairs. Virginia and Danny followed. Their feet clomped on the bare wooden steps.

"Papa? What's happening?" Virginia asked, but again she heard no answer.

In the cold kitchen, Papa said, "Danny, Ginny, Sarah, I'm taking you to Grandma Katie's for a day or two. I know you don't understand, but trust me. Everything will be okay, and I'll bring you home soon. Now let's say good-bye to Mama."

Papa led them into the bedroom. Mama was in the big oak bed. The lamplight shone on her pale face. Her hair, blonde touched with silver, fanned out on the pillow behind her. The children came to her, one by one. She hugged and kissed each of them.

Virginia whispered, "Are you sick, Mama?"

"No," said Mama, but her face was so pale and her voice so weak that Virginia felt a chill go down her back.

She thought Mama would tell them why they were leaving. Instead, Mama said, in a husky whisper, "Papa will take you to Grandpa Daniel's, just for a night or two.

"Now Danny, be good. Sarah, listen to Ginny. Ginny, you look out for Sarah. All of you, listen well to Grandma Katie. And show respect to Great-Grandma."

Mama always called her mother-in-law Grandma *Katie* for special things. So Mama was telling her something important. Virginia was sure that Mama meant more than the simple words.

Then Mama looked at Papa. Her face wrinkled. "Please hurry, Daniel!"

Virginia protested, "But, Mama, tomorrow's Christmas!"

Mama didn't answer. Her face was twisted. *What's wrong with Mama?* Virginia wondered. Her stomach knotted.

"Let's get going." Papa shooed them into the kitchen.

"I don't want to go with these dirty pants," objected Danny.

"Your pants don't matter," declared Papa. "Pull these pants on over your others. Hurry! We don't have a minute to waste."

He handed Danny pants that had been drying by the stove. Then he bundled Sarah up while Virginia put on boots, shawls, scarf, and mittens. Danny pulled on the clean pants, then his jacket and boots for the outdoors.

Papa opened the front door. Bells jingled on the waiting horses. Papa always used bells with the harness. He said they reminded the horses that they were at work. Now their big feet stomped restlessly. They were eager to be off.

Papa carried Sarah. Danny followed, then Virginia, across the new snow to the big bobsled

Papa had made from an old wagon bed. Papa nestled them in hay and tucked blankets all around them. Then, standing on the sled, he picked up the reins and clucked to the horses, Maude and Babe.

Virginia looked back at the barn, thinking of the animals asleep there: the five cows, the yearling colt, the dogs and cats, the hens and a rooster, the sheep, and the pigs. Especially, she thought of Ba-ba, her favorite sheep.

They were off to Grandma Katie's in the middle of the wintry night.

2

He Whistles!
She Sings!

The cold air cleared Virginia's head and brought her wide awake. It nipped her slightly upturned nose and made it numb. Warm breath steamed from her lips and froze on the mitten she held up to her nose.

The night was clean and crisp, with fields of unmarked, fresh-fallen snow. Up ahead, the moon made long tree shadows across the lane where they entered the hickory grove. The jingling of the bells, the *shushing* of the runners in the snow, and the heavy, fast plop-plop of the horses' feet—they all beat a rhythm in the still, still night.

In the hay, little Sarah slumped over, sound asleep. Virginia thought of Mama, alone in the big bed at home. *Why are we leaving her?*

She leaned over and asked Danny, "Why are we going to Grandma's?"

"I don't know," said Danny. His hair curled

from under his cap in dark rings.

As they slid smoothly along, Virginia thought about Grandma Katie's house. Usually, she loved to go there. She liked to help Grandma in the greenhouses. There, the smells of wood and coal burning in the stove mingled with the smells of the soil and growing plants.

Great-Grandma would be there, too. Getting old, she still moved around the house briskly. If they coaxed her a little, she might tell them a strange, wonderful story about when she was a little girl in Germany.

Then there would be Grandpa. He would show her something new he had learned—about a plant or an insect, or a machine he was inventing, or a new way to cook some familiar plant. Grandpa was the curious one, always experimenting, trying to see what would work. He called it "tinkering."

Best of all, it would be warm at Grandpa's place. On the coldest days of winter, it was warm. Keeping the greenhouses warm for the plants reminded Grandpa to keep the house warm, too. It never got as cold as Papa's house at night.

No, Virginia didn't mind going to Grandma Katie's. *If it weren't for Mama. . . .*

Virginia sighed. Spending Christmas at Grandpa's would be fun if only she knew what was happening at home.

The horses slowed to make the turn from their long lane onto the road. The sled slid smoothly around the corner. Papa sat on the bench and gave the horses free rein. He did not have to guide them. Maude and Babe had often gone to Grandpa's to work. They knew where they were going.

Papa began whistling.

How can Papa whistle? wondered Virginia. *Mama's at home in bed, and Papa's whistling while we're going farther and farther away from her. Mama had said to hurry. Papa doesn't hurry. How can we hurry more?*

Then Virginia sighed as she realized that the horses couldn't be hurried any faster on such a cold night. Papa was still whistling. Virginia loved to sing. Why not sing, too? She knew the words, so she sang with him,

Away in a manger, no crib for a bed,
The little Lord Jesus laid down his sweet head.
The stars in the bright sky looked down. . . .

Singing about the little Lord Jesus helped her forget Mama for a short time. She looked up. Those long-ago stars were still overhead.

"Do you have to sing?" growled Danny.

"No, but it's better than thinking."

"Some Christmas!" he grumped, his voice squeaking upward on the end of Christmas.

Virginia couldn't help thinking, *We'll miss the candy that's always on the table for us on Christmas morning.* She puzzled over what was happening. *Why are we going to Grandma Katie's in the middle of the night?*

21

Papa flicked the reins over horses' backs and gently urged them on. Then he kept whistling. His tune came back to Virginia, ending the song over and over:

The little Lord Jesus asleep on the hay!
The little Lord Jesus asleep on the hay!
The little Lord Jesus asleep on the hay!

She wondered, *Why does Papa whistle the same ending over and over?*

Virginia nestled deeper into the hay in the wagon bed. She thought about how the hay must have warmed the Lord Jesus just as it was warming her. A long time later, she noticed: *Papa is still whistling the ending, whistling the same ending over and over!*

3

Back to Bed

They were coming to Grandma Katie's. They rounded the bend in the road. By moonlight, Virginia saw the house, the barn, and the greenhouses. The horses broke into a dash and pulled right up to the yard gate.

"Whoa!" Papa called loudly as he pulled on the reins. Then he roared, "MAMA! PAPA!" He jumped off and tied the lines to a post. Again he shouted, "MAMA!" At last he seemed to remember Virginia and Danny and Sarah. He changed his shout to "GRANDMA KA-A-A-ATIE!"

Inside the house, a lamp glowed. Grandma Katie beckoned from the window.

Papa lifted Sarah from the sled and stood her in the snow. He gave Virginia a hand down, then picked up Sarah and carried her. Virginia followed, then Danny. The door opened. Grandma Katie pulled them in.

"Come in, come in," she welcomed them.

23

"Here, let me take your wraps."

"I must go right away," Papa told Grandma.

"Is everything fine? Is Christina well?" Grandma asked.

"She's well," Papa said, "but I have to fetch Samantha. Samantha won't be expecting me yet, so I'll have to wait for her to get ready. Please be good, Danny, Ginny, Sarah."

Then he hugged each one quickly, turned, and shut the door after him. They heard him call to the horses as he turned them around.

Virginia thought, *Samantha comes when folks are sick. Why will Papa fetch Samantha for Mama? Mama said she wasn't sick.*

Danny grumbled to himself in a low voice so Grandma wouldn't hear, "I don't know why we have to come here. Why couldn't we stay at home in bed?"

"Shhh!" Virginia hissed. "You'll make Grandma feel bad."

Grandma asked Danny to carry the lantern while she led Sarah up to bed. Virginia followed. Grandma tucked the two girls in while Danny waited at the door. Then he took the lantern to the next room and slipped into bed.

"Grandma, Mama said she wasn't sick," Virginia said. "Then why is Papa fetching Samantha?"

"Your Mama's not sick, but she needs a little help. Samantha will help your Mama."

"Help with what?" Virginia asked.

"Something," replied Grandma. "I can't tell

you yet. Your mama and papa will tell you. Children aren't told such things. You'll just have to wait and see."

Grandma Katie set the lantern in the hall and turned it down so it made a little light in both rooms. She pulled a chair into the hall with a scraping sound. Grandma sat down and began to sing,

Away in a manger, no crib for a bed . . .

The same song again! Virginia didn't really mind, though. She was glad Grandma cared enough to sit and sing for them. Virginia said silent prayers for Mama. She listened to Grandma sing until she felt warm and fuzzy inside. At last, she drifted into sleep.

4

Grandma Frowns

As Virginia woke in the morning, she was dreaming about the spelling bee. Every spring there was a spelling contest at school. She hoped to win the bee this year, her last year of school. Virginia had already started studying for it. She had a warm and pleasant feeling, just thinking about it.

Then she remembered she was at Grandma's. The warmth was real. The house was big and silent, but warm. Sarah was still asleep beside her. Virginia crept out of bed. The floor was smooth wood, cool but not ice-cold. She pulled on shoes and stockings and went downstairs.

Grandpa Daniel and Great-Grandma were at the table, eating breakfast, but Grandma was standing by the window. She was staring, with a frown on her face. *If Mama isn't sick, why does Grandma look so worried?*

Virginia coughed. Grandma whirled around. A smile replaced the frown.

"Merry Christmas!" she cried. She ran across the kitchen, swept Virginia into her arms, and gave her a big hug.

"Grandma, when can we go home?" Virginia asked. "I should help Mama get breakfast while Papa milks the cows. It's Christmas morning. Mama will make a special breakfast."

Grandma thought a bit, then she said, "Your mama will not make Christmas breakfast. She wants you to have a happy Christmas without her. Today she has to do the most important work in the whole world.

"When her work is over, Papa will come for you. She wants you to celebrate Jesus' birthday while she is working."

"But I don't understand. . . ."

Grandma put a finger on her lips. "Hush, Ginny. Have a little faith. You don't have to understand. Now sit down and eat your breakfast."

Just then, Sarah called, from the doorway, "Grandma, I'm awake. Is it Christmas?"

Sarah looked like a tiny Christmas angel in her long white nightgown and her blond hair tousled into a halo around her head.

"Yes, it's Christmas morning," Grandma replied. "We didn't know you children would be here for Christmas, so we don't have any candy for you, but we will make a celebration.

"Let's eat first. You like mush. I made some

just for you. Grandpa, don't you think you'd better wake Danny?"

Grandpa pulled up chairs and seated Sarah and Virginia while Grandma put their steaming mush into bowls. Then they waited for Danny while Grandpa went upstairs.

When Danny slid sleepily onto the bench behind the table, Grandpa asked a blessing on their food and a special Christmas blessing, too. Grandma passed a bowl of maple sugar and a pitcher of milk from their cows. The warm mush slid down Virginia's throat.

After breakfast, Grandma said, "Now, girls, time to get dressed."

Sarah and Virginia looked at each other in surprise.

"I—we—Papa didn't pack any clothes," Virginia said.

Grandma began to laugh, then Grandpa laughed. Great-Grandma began to laugh, too. Then Sarah and Virginia laughed. Even Danny forgot his gloom and laughed.

"We'll have to wear our nightgowns for Christmas Day!" Virginia said.

"That won't matter," Grandma told them. "Baby Jesus had no clothes. Mary and Joseph wrapped him in strips of cloth."

"How do you know he had no clothes?" Virginia asked.

"They wrapped him in swaddling clothes—just long strips of cloth wrapped tightly."

"Well, I'm glad I brought these extra pants,"

said Danny. "I'd smell like manure all Christmas Day if I hadn't. Why was Papa in such a rush anyway? He made me put on those dirty old pants beside the bed. It would have only taken a minute to find clean ones."

There was silence. Virginia sighed. How could Grandma be so stubborn? *Why won't she explain what's happening?*

Grandma began clearing the table and washing dishes. Sarah and Virginia helped. When the dishes were dried and put away, Grandma brushed out Sarah's hair. Then she gave Virginia a hairbrush. Virginia brushed until her hair was shiny and golden.

The girls put on their shoes and stockings. They had to stay dressed in their nightgowns. Virginia was glad Mama had made ruffles on the bottom of their nightgowns and nice bows at the neck.

Then Grandma announced, "We're going to make a maple cookie house. We have no molasses for a gingerbread house, but we have lots of maple sugar, so we'll use that. When your papa comes for you, you'll have something to take home for your mama. But first we must take care of the greenhouses."

5

Faith as a Lemon Seed

Virginia wanted to help Grandma and Grandpa in the greenhouses. Grandma said Danny could stay inside with Great-Grandma and watch Sarah since he didn't want to come along. She gave him the job of cleaning the lamp chimneys and trimming the wicks on the kitchen lamps.

Virginia loved being in the greenhouses. Today, Grandma had to water beds of lettuce and open the roof ventilators a crack. Grandpa was outside, chipping frozen coal loose from a big heap. Again and again he loaded the wheelbarrow. He dumped the loads inside by the furnace where the coal could thaw, dry, and warm up before it was needed. When he was finished, he would feed the fire.

Virginia asked to help water the lettuce. She filled a barrel on wheels with water from the stone trough in the packing room. Then she pushed it up and down the rows of lettuce,

ladling out water by the dipperful. By the time Grandma had the ventilators open, Virginia had finished watering the lettuce.

As always, Virginia stopped under the lemon tree to look up and wonder at the lemons that grew there. She knew of no other place where lemons grew. They reminded her that Grandma Katie had come from Germany with Grandpa Daniel long ago. Grandma Katie always said, *With faith as little as a lemon seed, you can do anything.*

Then she thought of her mother at home in bed. Her mother would say, *Yes, but—sometimes a spot of hard work will do nicely.* Was that what her mother, Christina, was doing today—*a spot of hard work?* What was a spot of hard work, anyhow?

Virginia also remembered what Great-Grandma always said: *Keep the faith and milk the cow!* Great-Grandma brought that saying from Germany. Virginia wasn't sure what that meant, either.

She had been looking up at the lemon tree for some time, lost in thought, when Grandma came by the tree.

"Oh, Grandma, let's make hot lemonade for Christmas!" suggested Virginia.

"That would be good with cookies," agreed Grandma. "We'll take some lemons along in." She got a short ladder, climbed up, and picked three ripe lemons. "These will do just fine!"

That afternoon, Grandma, Virginia, and

Sarah made cookies. Great-Grandma sat by, "supervising," as she called it.

Danny watched while they mixed the cookie dough, kneaded it, rolled it out, and cut out the cookies. Virginia knew he really wanted to help, but men didn't make cookies. Virginia thought that was silly. Yet she knew she couldn't change his mind. Danny's mind was not easy to change.

Grandma scooped more coal into the firebox that warmed the oven. When the temperature was right, they put the sides of the cookie house on flat trays and baked them. They made a roof and a chimney, too. At last, the pieces of the house were all cut. There was some dough left.

"Let's make cookies for the birds," said Grandma. They cut some long cookies and punched out a hole in the top. The hole was just right to thread ribbon through and hang the cookies in the spruce tree outside the window. There was a little more dough left.

"May we make the Baby Jesus?" asked Sarah. "This is his birthday, you know."

Soon Sarah and Virginia

had a row of fat little maple cookie babies. When the dough was all used up, Grandma put the babies on a tray and baked them in the oven, too.

While the last cookies baked, Grandma made hot lemonade. She put it in the special thin china cups that Grandpa had given her many Christmases ago.

Tangy and steamy, the lemonade was a good drink for pretending. Virginia could imagine herself a rich lady or a queen, sipping lemonade daintily from the delicate cup. Today she daydreamed that she was Miss Virginia, a rich lady who never had to work, especially not on Christmas.

When the cookies were cool, they put ribbon through the holes in the ones for the birds. Grandpa hung them outside in the spruce tree while they watched from the window. Birds soon came and began pecking at the cookies.

Sarah called, "Grandma, look! The tree has moving decorations!"

She was right. The birds, especially the red cardinals, flashed their colors through the evergreen tree. Grandpa and Danny watched with the girls, too. Even Great-Grandma left her rocker to join them at the window. "Feed the birds, and you'll bring the spring!" she said.

"I hope so!" Virginia replied.

Soon it was time to put the maple cookie house together. Grandma made icing. They spread some icing on a wooden cutting board, then used the icing as glue to put the house together, piece by piece.

At last, the house was built and complete. It had snow on the roof and paper cut-out windows with cookie shutters, a door, and a friendly snowman in the yard.

"Grandma, why do you make cookie houses for Christmas?" asked Sarah as they cleaned up the kitchen.

Grandma stopped washing dishes. "Anything goes with Christmas if families do it together from love, to celebrate Jesus' birth. I think—"

"Grandma," Sarah broke in, "I wish Papa would come for us. I have to go home to Mama. She didn't have us or a cookie house for Christmas. I don't see why she has to do important work on Christmas day."

"I don't understand either," replied Grandma, "but it's God's work. That I can promise you. It's God's work!"

Grandma lit the lamp as soon as Grandpa left the house for evening milking. Daylight was ending with new fresh snow falling from a thick gray sky.

Cold frosted the kitchen windows. Sarah, looking for Papa any minute, kept a small circle of glass melted with her breath. Even Grandma peeped through that circle from time to time as she cut vegetables for a large pot of soup on the stove.

Grandma is worried, Virginia thought. *All*

day she frowns when she thinks we don't notice. Now she's frowning into the vegetable soup! Papa should be here by now.

"It's taking longer than you thought, isn't it?" Virginia asked Grandma.

"Yes." She gave Virginia a sharp look, then added, "But no news is good news."

Virginia puzzled over that, trying to imagine what bad news would be. But she couldn't think of anything because she didn't know what Mama was doing.

6

Three for Christmas!

When Papa burst in the door, the whole outdoors tried to come in with him. Snow swirled
around the kitchen table, where they were just
ready to eat. He slammed the door. By the look
on his face, they knew he had big news.

"Mama's okay. There are three of them!
Three of them! Think of it! We need you,
Grandma Katie. Can you come with us? Three
of them! Just think of it! Three of them!"

What was Papa talking about? Virginia felt
confused.

"Three! *Three!*" Grandma stood there with
her mouth open, astonished.

"*Three!*" echoed Grandpa. He pulled his
beard as he always did when he was surprised.

"Three of what?" Virginia asked Papa.

"What will you do with them? Are they all
alive?" asked Grandma.

"They're all alive, but one's mighty little."

"Three of what?" Virginia fairly screamed. Would they never pay attention to her? She thought she'd burst if they didn't tell her soon.

"Babies!" he said. "Babies!"

Danny, Virginia, and Sarah all drew in their breaths at once. Sarah's eyes were like soup bowls.

"Didn't anyone tell you yet?" asked Papa. He looked at Grandma. "Mama, I thought you'd tell them. I thought you'd explain."

For the second time, Grandma's mouth opened in surprise. She protested, "But, Daniel, it was so early for a baby and. . . ."

She didn't need to finish because Papa was talking to the children. "Your Mama was having a baby, but it turned out to be three babies. How do you like that!"

Papa picked up Sarah and gave her a swing around the room, then gave Virginia a whirl, too! Virginia had never seen him so excited. He might have swung Danny, too, if Danny hadn't stood with his hands crossed in front of him. Only his grin showed that he was excited, too!

"Can you come?" Papa asked Grandma again.

"Of course, Daniel. Let me take this soup along. I'll be ready in a few minutes."

Grandma picked up their full, untouched bowls of soup and dumped them back in the pot.

Sarah and Virginia rushed for their shawls. Even Danny was dressed and ready to go in a flash. The three of them were at the door and waiting before the grown-ups were ready.

Grandpa said, "I'll have to go, too! I'll take our sleigh so I can come home again. Your Grandma will want to stay a day or two, and I must keep the greenhouses for her. But I want to see those babies. Great-Grandma will be okay for several hours. It's good and warm in here."

Great-Grandma was dancing excitedly from one foot to the other. "Oh, no, Daniel! You're not letting me out of this. Not when I'm a triple Great-Grandma! I'm going along. *Three babies!* Think of it! I'll dress up warm."

Soon Great-Grandma was seated beside Danny on Grandpa's little cutter. This light sleigh had only one wide seat. It glided easily over the snow, pulled by one horse. It wasn't homemade like Papa's bobsled.

They packed the full kettle of soup in the back of the sled, the cookie house under the seat, and then got in—first Grandma, then Sarah, then Virginia. They were headed home. The sleigh bells seemed to jingle, *Three babies, three babies, three babies!*

Virginia turned around to see Grandpa, Great-Grandma, and Danny following in the cutter. She listened for his sleigh bells, but couldn't hear any. Maybe Grandpa's horse had none. Papa was the only man she knew who loved sleigh bells. Virginia loved them, too!

Virginia stuck out her tongue in the dark and caught snowflakes on it. *What will we do with three babies? Babies need to be held. Mama can't hold them all. Will Grandma hold one? Will they let me hold one?*

Her back was warm from leaning against the kettle of soup. Sarah leaned against it, too, so their backs were to each other. Virginia thought of the cookie house wrapped in oilcloth, under Papa's seat.

Papa was whistling the same song again,

I love thee, Lord Jesus!
Look down from the sky,
and stay by my cradle
till morning is nigh!

This time Virginia thought different words, changing them in her head until they said, *And stay by the babies till morning is nigh!* She could hardly believe it! *Three babies! I can't imagine three babies! No one else I know has ever had three babies!*

Snow was falling fast now. A wind kicked the flakes into her face and made them sting her cold cheeks. The horses hurried to get home.

7

Fitting in a Teacup

When they arrived at home, Papa and Grandpa carried the soup and the cookie house inside. Plump Samantha met them at the door with a fat finger to her lips. She had a habit of saying "so" as she started to speak. "So! Shut the door quickly so the babies don't get cold."

They shut the door, but Papa said he and Danny would tend to the horses before they took off their coats. Virginia could tell by the look on Danny's face that he wanted to see the babies first, but he didn't complain.

Papa and Danny went back out to take the horses to the barn. The minute they were gone, Virginia asked, "Where are they?" Her eyes were on the chairs in front of the stove, but she didn't dare run to them. She could hardly hold in her excitement.

Samantha motioned to the stove. The oven door was open. In front of the oven was a large pillow, resting on two facing chairs. Samantha said, "On the pillow."

Virginia quickly tiptoed across the room. The babies! All she could see were three tiny, wrinkled red faces. *How ugly!* she thought.

Grandma must have guessed what she was thinking. "Virginia, newborn babies are red and wrinkled and not very pretty. In a couple days, they'll look much better."

When Sarah had been born, Virginia didn't remember her looking ugly. She hadn't had much chance to see Sarah close up, because Mama had taken care of her. Virginia had been a little girl herself then.

The triplets were wrapped together in one blanket. Virginia asked Samantha, "Are they wrapped in swaddling clothes?"

Samantha looked surprised. "So, I guess you could say that. I wrapped them together because they are used to each other. They are too tiny for real clothes."

"Are they boys or girls?" Virginia asked. Papa had said there was just one girl, but she asked anyway, to be sure.

"Two boys and a girl," Samantha said. "So, the boys are so little that a teacup will fit right over their heads! That's really little. So, we tried to weigh them on the scale. So, together, the three of them—they weigh about ten pounds."

"May I hold one?" Virginia asked.

"So, not yet," replied Samantha. She mumbled something to herself, then added, "So, I should warn you. These babies are really too little to be born.

"First they should have more time to grow. But they got crowded with three of them, so they were born early. So they will probably not all live. We will have to handle them very carefully or none of them will live."

Virginia looked at the babies. Suddenly, they looked much prettier. She didn't want any of them to die, especially not the tiniest one.

Grandma was talking to Samantha. "Does Daniel know?" she asked.

Samantha shrugged. Her double chin shook when she answered, "So, he knows they were born too early, but he is so excited he hasn't thought about it yet."

"What are their names?" asked Sarah.

"Don't have any yet," replied Samantha. Think of names. You can help name them. So, now you want to see your mama, don't you? She is very tired. Birthing babies is hard work."

"The most important work in the world?" Virginia asked.

"That's what I said," Grandma agreed.

When they entered the bedroom, Mama was resting in the big bed with her eyes closed. Her face looked white against the pillow. She opened her eyes and smiled.

"Sarah. Virginia." Her voice was faint. Virginia and Sarah both kissed her. Then she closed her eyes and seemed to go to sleep.

Grandma waved for them to tiptoe out. They

left quietly.

"Will Mama get better?" asked Virginia, anxiously.

"Sure, the Lord willing," said Grandma.

Virginia wished she hadn't asked. "The Lord willing" sounded as though the Lord might not want her to get better.

"So, now you want to hold a baby?" asked Samantha as soon as they left the bedroom.

"Yes!" said Sarah and Virginia together. Virginia was relieved to forget about Mama for now.

"Then you may hold the girl. She's the biggest."

"The girl is the biggest!" Virginia was surprised.

"Yes, the girl is the biggest and the strongest," said Samantha.

8

Naming

Later, they were eating bowls of vegetable soup when Sarah announced, "The girl baby will be *Lucy*."

Papa put his spoon down and looked at Sarah, surprised. "What a good idea! I know Christina will like that." Sometimes Papa called Mama by her name, Christina.

"A-a-a-and," Sarah strung out the word, "I think the biggest boy will be *Laban*, and the littlest one will be *Tiny*."

"Now wait a minute," said Papa. "Laban is a name, but I've never in my life heard of a boy named Tiny. How would it sound for a man to be named Tiny?"

Papa was frowning. Then his face cleared. "I like Laban! Not everybody has a name like Laban, but Tiny! No, we won't call him Tiny. You'll have to do better than that! Think again."

"Well," said Sarah reluctantly. "I wanted

45

Tiny, but I'll call him Louis for Uncle Louis."

"Great!" said Papa. "If your Mama agrees, they will be Lucy, Laban, and Louis."

"So, the littlest one *should* be named Tiny," said Samantha, her chins wobbling, "because he will still be tiny if he lives. And you might be planning how to feed him. Christina will likely not have milk for three babies. Two babies, maybe. But not three."

"What do we do, then?" Virginia asked in dismay.

"Boil cow's milk, cool it to body heat, and try to feed him. But it doesn't always work."

When they finished eating, it was already late. Grandpa and Great-Grandma put on their heavy outside clothes. When they got home, they would have to fix fires in the house and the greenhouses. Soon they were gone.

Papa took a bowl of soup to Mama on a tray. He was still with her when they heard the first "Wah-ah-wah" from the babies. Sarah and Virginia hurried over to the pillow to look at them. The biggest one was crying loudly, but the other two squirmed and then began to whimper.

"So, what do you think?" Samantha whispered to Grandma. Her voice seemed strange, as though she was telling a secret.

Virginia listened. She watched Samantha and Grandma and saw them looking at each other. They seemed to be talking without words.

"So, we must decide," said Samantha. "Christina is not well enough."

Grandma's face frowned more than Virginia had ever seen her frown. Virginia knew she was trying to decide something important. *What is it? What can be so important that Grandma is so upset?*

At last, Grandma said, "I think the two biggest ones—Lucy and Laban. They have the best chance. Let's try to feed Louis ourselves."

"What do you mean? What are you talking about?" Virginia asked. Her back was to the warm stove. She was watching Louis's tiny wrinkled face. No one answered.

Samantha carried baby Lucy and Grandma carried baby Laban to Mama. Sarah followed them, leaving little Louis in the kitchen alone with Virginia. She stood over him and patted him ever so gently.

Papa came out of the bedroom, and his face was serious. He looked like he might cry. Virginia had never seen him look so sober.

Suddenly she knew why Grandma had frowned and why Papa was sober. There was something terrifying about the thoughts that went through her head. She didn't want to think them, but she couldn't stop them.

Virginia knew Grandma and Samantha had just decided that Lucy and Laban would get Mama's milk.

Grandma and Samantha have picked Lucy and Laban because they are biggest and strongest. Louis is so tiny that they don't expect him to live anyway.

Suddenly, she was angry. *I can feed Louis,* she fumed to herself. *I will learn how to fix his milk. I will learn how to feed him. I have to learn or Louis won't live.*

Grandma and Samantha will go home soon. There will be no one else but Papa and Danny and Sarah and me. Papa has all the cows to care for, and he needs Danny's help. Sarah is too little. It will be up to me! I must save Louis! I must!

By the time Grandma returned, Virginia had made up her mind. "Grandma Katie, you must teach me how to fix cow's milk for Tiny. You must show me how to feed him."

"His name is Louis, and you're too young. . . ." Grandma paused, then ended with a rush, "You're too young to have the duty of feeding Louis."

"Then who?"

Grandma Katie looked at Virginia with serious eyes. "You're right. There will be no one else. You will have to do it, and I have to teach you how."

Then she muttered to herself, "And I don't know how either, not really!"

Grandma Katie didn't know how to fix the milk! Suddenly, Virginia was filled with panic! No one knew how to fix the milk. She suspected that not even Samantha, who knew almost everything, knew how to fix the milk for this baby. She would have to do it herself.

Virginia wasn't used to praying in the middle of the kitchen with other people around her.

But now she *needed* to say a prayer. She looked up at the ceiling and hoped God wouldn't mind that she didn't close her eyes. Then she prayed, clearly, in her mind, *God, no one knows how to feed Tiny. Help me feed him, please. Please! Help me save Tiny. Amen.*

There! Her best prayer was said. She had asked and prayed it loud and clear for God to hear—loud in her head, anyhow. If God didn't answer right away, she was sure God was willing. Wasn't *the Lord willing?* Why wouldn't God want to save Tiny?

Tiny! Tiny! She had forgotten and called him Tiny in her prayer. She was just feeling sad for having made a mistake, when she had a wonderful thought: *Louis is Tiny, and God loves him! It is good to be Tiny that way.*

She began singing softly, "I love thee, Lord Jesus! Look down from the sky. . . ." Suddenly, Tiny's red, ugly face was beautiful. He wailed in a thin high voice that sounded as weak as a newborn kitten's. But he was beautiful!

"Grandma, I'm ready for my first feeding lesson," Virginia said.

9

Feeding

Grandma says the milk must boil for several minutes. Then it must sit till it's cool enough for Tiny to drink it.

Virginia had boiled the milk, and now the pan of hot milk was cooling, sitting in a bigger pan of cold water. Tiny was still crying. She went to the pillow and picked him up.

He was so tiny that his body wasn't much longer than her hand. He made small mewing sounds and turned his head toward her, as though he were trying to find milk.

"Soon we'll have something for you, Tiny," she whispered soothingly in his ear. Then she had to put him down to check the milk.

She dipped in a spoon and brought it out of the warm milk with a cry of dismay. "Look! There's a big scum on top. Now what do I do?"

"Throw the scum away," said Grandma calmly. "There's plenty left under the scum."

When that was done, Grandma instructed, "Now drip some of the warm milk on your wrist to make sure it's not too hot."

Virginia did that, licked it off, and reported that it felt safe. "Now, how can I feed it to him?"

Just then, Samantha came back with a baby on each arm. Again without words, the two women seemed to speak to each other across the room. Samantha shook her head.

Virginia saw Grandma nod. Were they "talking" about the babies being fed again? Virginia didn't understand.

"So, I'd advise against it," said Samantha. "It would be better for two babies to be healthy than for three to be hungry."

Virginia looked into the pan of milk so they wouldn't see the tears in her eyes. *They aren't going to give Tiny a chance to drink Mama's milk. Mama is so tired she won't even know if they give Tiny a turn or not. She probably doesn't know how little Tiny is.*

He is the tiniest baby. Maybe the tiniest one in the whole world right now. I haven't fed him yet, and he'll probably die. No, he won't! I won't let him! I won't let him! I won't let him die!

Aloud, Virginia asked Grandma again, "Now, how can I feed the milk to Tiny? Show me how."

"Pour some of the milk into a dish and set it on the table. Bring your smallest spoon and a cloth for wiping any spills." Grandma gently picked up Louis and carried him to a chair beside the table.

Grandma held the baby on her lap, with a folded towel under his head. She squeezed his cheeks a little with her left thumb and forefinger, to pry open his mouth. With her right hand, she took a few drops of milk on the spoon and dribbled them into his mouth.

He sputtered, and Grandma wiped his face softly. Virginia bent over and watched intently. Next time, she would feed him just like Grandma was doing. But Grandma didn't wait for the next time.

"Here, Virginia. You can do this as well as I. You might as well try your hand at it. Too bad we don't have a feeding bottle. Maybe Papa can get one tomorrow."

Carefully, Virginia held the baby just as Grandma had done. He made soft sucking sounds, but he had nothing to suck. Yet he had learned to open his lips a crack. Soon Virginia was spooning milk into Tiny's mouth, a few drops at a time.

At last, the baby was being fed. After a while, with much sputtering and gulping, Louis was full and fast asleep. She put him with the other two.

Suddenly there was a sound from the babies. Virginia hurried over to look. Louis had vomited the milk out and was lying with his head in it.

"Oh, no!" cried Virginia. "You spit it all up! What will we do now?"

Right away Danny appeared at her side.

"Let me help, Ginny. I'll wash up the baby while you fix more milk." He took the tiny baby from her. He began unwrapping him carefully, talking to him all the while.

Virginia looked in wonder at her brother, handling the baby so well. Was this the same Danny as the grumpy brother she had known the last few weeks? She didn't have time to think about it much, though. She was wondering what to do next.

"Grandma," Virginia said anxiously, "What do we do now?"

"What do we do, Samantha?" asked Grandma, passing on the question.

With a sinking feeling, Virginia realized that even Grandma didn't know what to do. Samantha was thoughtful but did not have one clear cure. She just said they should experiment to see what would work.

"So, we could try a little water in the milk. Maybe it's too strong for him. We could try a little sugar in it. Or we could put in a little whiskey."

"Whiskey!" Ginny exclaimed.

"Yes, whiskey. It's a medicine when used this way. Whiskey might pull the baby through the night. But I doubt that he'll make it.

"This time, Ginny, don't try to get the baby full. Just feed him a little, then wait, then a little more. Feed him only a little at a time, but a lot of times."

"I'll help," Danny volunteered.

He held the tiny infant in one arm, cupped close to his body.

Virginia got the milk she had boiled from the back porch, where it had been put to cool. She poured out a small dishful, put in a little water, then added a spoonful of sugar.

Samantha stood watching her, a dull look on her face. Then she said, "I hope you aren't getting all taken up with this baby. I have never in my life seen such a little one. Lots of bigger ones have died. So I just don't want you to be too sad when he doesn't make it."

Virginia's temper flared. "Well, of course he won't live if you don't think he will. You wouldn't even feed him, if it were up to you. Would you now?"

Samantha shrugged. "Maybe not," she admitted. "So if I saw I couldn't take care of a baby, and it didn't have a chance, I might not try. Well, yes, I would. I couldn't stand to starve anything. But I'd give the baby just its fair share of mothering, and no more.

"So you don't realize yet what you've set out to do. You'll have to feed this baby, hour after hour after hour, for a long time. Oh well, *you're* the one doing it, not me.

"So you might as well add a little whiskey to that milk. Just a drop or two. Enough to calm the baby's stomach so he keeps the milk down."

Virginia knew where Papa kept the whiskey. She knew her parents kept it there for medicine, but she had never seen them use it. Now she opened the door to the china cupboard and took out the small bottle hidden behind the dishes. *Grandma wants to see if I do it right,* she thought. Virginia poured out half a spoonful.

"Like this?" she asked.

"Not that much. Only a few drops . . . like this." Samantha took away the spoon and added about three drops of whiskey to the dish of milk.

Virginia tested the milk on her wrist again, to see if it was warm and not hot. At last the precious milk was ready.

"I'll feed him this time," offered Danny.

However, now the baby was sleeping. First Danny and then Virginia tried to waken him. Even Sarah took a turn at tickling his feet. But the baby's mouth would not open.

Then Virginia tried squeezing his cheeks, as Grandma had done. A tiny pucker opened between his lips. They managed to feed Tiny a few spoonfuls of milk.

Then they gave up, wrapped the baby warmly, and put him in front of the fire with the other two. Long ago those bigger ones had received another feeding and were sleeping peacefully on the pillow.

10

Wonderful Home!

In the kitchen, Virginia awoke from an uneasy sleep in the big soft love seat. Danny was fixing the fire. Usually, they let it go out at night and lit it again in the morning. But now they had to keep the fire going all the time.

She glanced at the clock and saw it was 2:00 a.m. It had been five hours since Tiny had eaten. By now, he should have been awake and crying for food.

Quickly Virginia went to the pillow by the stove and picked the baby up. The tiny lips looked blue. She held him close to her face to see if he had any breath. Virginia felt a faint puff of air and breathed a sigh of relief.

She put Louis down and went to the back porch for milk that had been boiled. Virginia measured a small amount into a bowl, then added a little water and sugar.

By then, Danny had finished fixing the fire.

She set the bowl on the stove to warm the milk a little. Then she added three drops of whiskey, just as Samantha had showed her.

"I'll squeeze his cheeks this time," Danny volunteered.

Virginia spooned a drop or two at a time into his tiny mouth. "I wish we had something else to feed him with. A spoon sure is hard to use for feeding a baby."

Neither of them spoke much as they fed Louis. She and Danny were doing much better with the feeding. One of them would press his cheeks until his mouth opened, then the other would dribble in the milk. They would wait to be sure he had swallowed it before giving him more.

They had just put Louis back in bed when little Lucy and Laban woke, both crying lustily. Samantha came into the kitchen, changed their diapers, and took them to their mother to be fed.

When she returned to the kitchen, Virginia said, "Samantha, I need to know how to change diapers. We haven't changed Tiny's diaper yet."

"So, he isn't Tiny!" scolded Samantha. "Now, now! You should know how to change a diaper. You're a big girl. So, you do it like this."

She gathered up Louis and showed Virginia and Danny how to change the diaper.

"Enough of lessons in the night," she said. "Now go back to sleep and get some rest before that baby needs you again. It will be morning before you know it."

Virginia settled back into the love seat in the kitchen corner. Danny put more wood on the fire before lying down on the woodbox behind the stove. Samantha brought Lucy and Laban back and tucked them in. Then she blew out the lantern and left the kitchen.

Virginia lay there thinking about the long Christmas Day that had just passed. They had hardly celebrated Christmas, yet there had been something holy and wonderful about it. There had been no candy. But with three real babies asleep before the fire, who needed other gifts?

The lights were out. Only a red glow showed through the door of the firebox. The smells of wood smoke and oil mingled with the smells of soap and diapers.

Virginia lay there thinking, *This is home. My wonderful home. My family. Our babies. Thank you, God. Amen.*

She was sound asleep.

11

To Find a Bottle

The next day, Papa hitched up the horses. He set out to buy a feeding bottle and nipple. The store was eight miles away, so Virginia knew he wouldn't be back for several hours.

All morning, her mind was with Papa, imagining him telling the storekeeper about the three babies. She could hardly wait for his return. The day dragged on.

They settled into a routine: Half an hour to feed Tiny. An hour and a half for him to sleep. Then it was time to feed him again. Samantha said if there was a chance for him to live, that was how often they needed to feed him.

Virginia was glad Danny was helping her. Grandma Katie watched them feed Tiny, but she didn't help. She said it was better if they got used to feeding him right away.

Papa came home at five o'clock. His shoulders were hunched forward. His eyes had deep wrinkles around them. "I got a bottle," he said, "but no sucking part. After supper, I'll try to make a nipple."

"Make one!" exclaimed Virginia.

"The sucking part is made of leather, anyway. I'll try using my new gloves," said Papa. Virginia's heart did a flip-flop. Papa's new gloves! The ones he was saving for a special time!

After supper, Papa got out his gloves, a needle, and a knife. Virginia sat down to watch. Working with care, he cut off a finger and pulled it down over the neck of the bottle. It was a good fit.

Then he removed the finger, held the needle over a flame until it was red hot, and burned a small hole in the end of the finger. Last, he cut some string for tying the homemade nipple around the bottle.

The next feeding, Virginia tried to use the new feeding bottle. Louis wrinkled his tiny face and sputtered and choked. At last, Virginia gave up using the bottle. She and Danny fed him as before, with a spoon.

Papa shook his head. "I declare, that baby is going to be a spoon-fed baby from birth.

I give up! You seem to be doing just fine with him. Too bad I ruined my glove! Maybe we can sew it together again."

Another night and day passed. At times they began to see Mama now, though she seemed to be living in a daze. She would come out to get a drink of water and then go back to bed.

Once she stopped to look at the babies. They heard her make a choking sound. She was standing with one hand over her mouth. "The third one is so little!" she cried.

"So, he is little," Samantha agreed.

"Do I only feed the two bigger ones?"

"That's right," said Samantha. "So, we decided to give you the two heavier babies to feed. Danny and Virginia have been feeding the smallest one."

"I'd think the littlest one would need me most," Mama observed. "Three babies! I still can't believe I had three babies! And this one so tiny."

"He's so little his head will fit in a teacup," Danny said.

Mama was sniffling back tears. "I feel so badly that I can't feed Louis too. I thought you were giving the babies turns or something. Oh, I don't know what I thought. I've been in a fog. I just didn't know Louis was getting *nothing*."

Virginia tried to ease her mother's pain. "He seems to recognize us already."

"The children are doing fine, feeding him,"

said Grandma Katie.

Mama smiled through her tears. "I'm sure they are. Ginny, of course you are taking good care of Louis. I know you are doing your best. Even if he dies, you still did your best. If he lives, you and God will have done a miracle."

"And Danny," added Virginia, wanting to be fair to her brother.

A miracle! Is this what a miracle is? This miracle takes a lot of hard work. I thought a miracle was something easy, like ta-da, God changes water into wine. I wish God would change cow's milk into mother's milk. Now, that would be a real miracle.

Again, Virginia was busy preparing more milk for Louis. She left out the whiskey, now that the baby was keeping the milk down.

Danny had come in. He picked up Tiny and talked to him. Once more they settled down to feed him. It was Danny's turn to squeeze his cheeks while Virginia dribbled milk in his mouth.

12

Visitors

Three days after the babies were born, visitors began to come. They arrived in sleighs and sleds and buggies and carriages. Everyone for miles around seemed to have heard that triplets were born. They all came to see for themselves.

Each person had an excuse. Mrs. Anderson said, "I just came to bring you a cake. I know you can use it, seeing as how you're so busy with three babies." Mr. Anderson stood, holding his hat, while the two Anderson children looked at the babies.

Grandma welcomed the visitors. But Virginia could tell, by the little wrinkle in her forehead, that she was not pleased. Would the babies catch some illness from the visitors?

Virginia hovered over the triplets, watching that the children didn't try to pick them up. Mama came from the bedroom to greet her visitors. She sat down in the love seat by the fire.

Grandma sat down, too.

The three women talked in hushed voices. One of the children asked to hold the baby, but Mrs. Anderson said no.

Soon they were gone. An hour later, another sleigh arrived. This time, old Mrs. Stone said, "Here's a little jelly I thought would taste good while the Mrs. is recovering."

She handed Virginia a jar. Her son, who also seemed old, had brought her. Now he stood by while she looked at the babies. She made clicking noises with her tongue and cooed, but the babies slept on.

"I've seen a lot of babies in my day, but these are the littlest babies I've ever seen. Live babies, that is. And it's the only time I've seen triplets. I guess we'd best be going. Where's your mother?"

"In bed," said Virginia.

"Well, I'll just go back and say good-bye," said Mrs. Stone. She marched toward the bedroom. Virginia heard talking. Then Mrs. Stone came out.

Soon the Stones were gone. Virginia set out some food for lunch. Before they ate, she put water on the stove to heat for washing dishes. After they had eaten, Virginia was starting to wash dishes when Miss Molly arrived. She drove her own horse. Everyone knew her as a stubborn old lady who lived alone.

Miss Molly handed Virginia a paper and said, "This is Great-Aunt Edith's recipe for mus-

tard plaster in case you need it for the babies. It's good for all kinds of sickness."

She bent over the babies, then pulled the wrapping loose on the biggest one to look at its hands. She frowned, and then smiled.

"This one will be rich," she said.

"How do you know?" asked Virginia.

"Lines in the hands," said Miss Molly. "Now let me help you with the dishes."

She rolled up her sleeves and began washing pots and pans. When the dishes were done, she put on her bonnet and shawl.

"Say hello to your Mama for me," she said as she went out the door.

All day long, visitors came and went. Each time the door opened, cold air rushed in. Danny and Virginia and even little Sarah guarded the door, shutting it quickly before the kitchen had a chance to cool off.

By evening, Tiny had developed a little cough which worried Virginia. He sounded so weak when he coughed. Each time she picked him up, Virginia tried to guess if he was gaining weight. He always seemed the same.

13

Waiting to Bee

It was nearly time for Christmas vacation to be over. School would begin again. During the winter, Papa usually took them to school in the sleigh. On sunny afternoons, they walked home from school.

Virginia could hardly wait for the spelling bee. She was a good speller. This year, as one of the three oldest students, she thought she might have a chance to win the bee.

On the evening before the first day of school, Papa called Virginia into the kitchen.

"Virginia," he said, "I want you to finish school, but I don't see how Mama can handle the babies without you. Would you stay home till summer and help with them? It will be for only a few months. Then you can finish in the fall."

Virginia had a sinking feeling in her stomach. She wanted to be in the spelling bee. She didn't want to stay home, but she knew Papa was right. Mama couldn't handle the babies without her. She would have to stay home.

Tears filled her eyes. Papa noticed. "I'm so sorry, Virginia. I know you want to go to school. But you love the babies, too, and they need a lot of care."

"It's just that I wanted to win the spelling bee," she said.

The next day started out being long and lonely. After Danny went to cut wood with Papa and Sarah went to school, Virginia dripped tears onto Tiny's face as she fed him.

Then, in the afternoon, more visitors came. Soon she was so busy taking care of Tiny and letting people in and out that she didn't have time to think about being lonely.

By that evening, the kitchen was full of food brought by guests. There were cookies, bread, cake, canned pears, green beans, corn, tomato juice, ham, and smoked sausage.

Tiny seemed to be getting weaker, Virginia thought. But she wasn't sure. She was often tired from losing sleep at night to feed Tiny and check on the babies.

The following Saturday, Samantha went home at last. Virginia felt lost when she left. Samantha had told her how to take care of the babies. Now she was afraid that something would happen to them without Samantha there to help her.

After the noon meal, Sarah napped on the

woodbox beside the stove. Papa dozed in the soft, old love seat. Mama had fed babies Lucy and Laban.

Before long, Danny and Virginia were feeding Tiny again. They tried to think of ways to make Tiny healthier as they fed him.

Virginia was in despair. "What can he eat?"

"You can't feed him anything but milk, can you?" asked Danny.

"I don't know. He seems weaker and weaker. I don't think he's getting enough to eat. If I could only think of something that he could eat that wouldn't make him sick."

Suddenly Tiny coughed. It was a feeble, tired cough. Virginia picked him up. She held him upside down and patted his back. Thick mucus came out of his throat. She took her finger, put it in his mouth, and wiped out more mucus.

"We won't dare leave him alone for a minute tonight." Virginia's voice was determined. "If we do, he'll have this thick stuff in his throat and choke to death before we know it.

"You'd better get some sleep, Danny. I'll take the first watch till midnight. Then you can watch until two, and I'll watch until four. We'll just take turns like that through the night."

Grandma came into the kitchen, and Virginia showed her the thick mucus in Tiny's throat. Grandma said, "Well, they don't usually live long after the mucus starts. Really, Virginia, there's not much you can do. He'll probably be dead by morning. I'm sorry. I truly am.

"There, now, don't cry." Grandma hugged her.

Virginia *was* crying so much that tears splashed down on Tiny's face. She was glad when Grandma went away. But she didn't put Tiny down. She laid him on her lap, stomach down, and gently patted his back for the next two hours. That removed more of the thick mucus.

Papa came in from doing the chores at the barn. He had something under his arm. When he put it down, they could see that it was a tiny lamb. "Ba-ba had her lamb early. It's too little, like our babies. Well, I guess there's room for one more in this kitchen. Do you want to feed it, too, Ginny?" Papa was cheerful.

"Papa," Virginia protested, "how can you even ask me? Tiny is so sick, and I've been holding him for two hours. I don't see how I can take care of another thing.

"Tiny needs me, Papa. He'll die if I don't take care of him. A baby is more important than a lamb."

"I'll feed it!" volunteered Sarah. "I'd like to feed it. I have nothing to take care of like the rest of you."

"Fine!" agreed Papa. "You can take care of Ba-ba's lamb. What will you call it?"

"I think I'll call it Babette," said Sarah.

14

Ask the Minister

Virginia was so tired she could have slept standing up. Another day and a long night had gone by. In the morning, Grandpa came for Grandma.

Before she left, Grandma told Virginia, "You've been doing a wonderful job with Tiny. Don't blame yourself if he dies. No one could have done any better than you."

Grandma's words made Virginia feel good, knowing she was doing a good job. But they made her sad, too. She didn't want to think of Tiny dying.

After Grandma left, Virginia and Danny stood looking at the babies. Lucy and Laban were growing and contented.

"Tiny looks like a skinny old man," said Danny.

There was a knock at the door. Virginia opened it and welcomed the minister and his wife, beaming with joy. They didn't know how Virginia and Danny felt.

To Virginia, it seemed that only she and Danny worried about the littlest baby. Yet Mother was up and caring for them all as well as she could. Now that both Grandma and Samantha had gone home, the real work of caring for the babies had just begun.

While the minister and his wife oh'ed and ah'ed over the babies, Virginia stood inside the bedroom door, feeling hot tears scald her cheeks. What could she do about Tiny?

Suddenly she had an idea: *Ask the minister. He should have answers. He always has answers on Sunday morning in church. Why not now?*

She crept out of the bedroom and joined her mother and Danny and Sarah. Then she waited for a lull in the talking. There it was! She took a deep breath and asked, "Do you know what we can feed Tiny? Cow's milk isn't right for him. He's going to die unless we find something else to feed him soon."

"Oh, my!" exclaimed the minister, in the huge silence that followed. "Is that true?"

"I'm afraid so," admitted Mama in a tired voice.

"Well, I've heard that goat's milk is good," the minister's wife suggested.

"But where do we get goat's milk?" asked Mama.

"I really don't know. Now, Norman, don't

you think it's time we are going? We shouldn't have stayed this long, with the babies so little and all."

They got up to leave. The minister turned back on his way out. "God bless you with help in finding a goat."

"Thank you," they called back. Tears were running down Virginia's cheeks. Danny was nowhere about. He had quietly slipped out to the barn while they were talking.

When Papa came in from the barn that night, he had good news for Virginia. "Your teacher stopped to see me this evening. Sarah told him how disappointed you are that you can't be in the spelling bee. He says there is no reason you can't be in the bee.

"You can study at home. We'll get someone to come and help with the babies the night of the bee. Would you like that, Virginia?"

"Oh, yes, Papa!" Virginia exclaimed. "I'll study hard."

She found a dictionary and began to study that very evening.

15

Oat Porridge

Papa was busy at the barn. It seemed that everything had decided to give birth at once. Maidy the cow had a new calf, the contrary little hen had hatched three black chicks, and one of the horses had a new colt. Papa tried to help at the house with the babies. But all the animals kept him busy at the barn.

Virginia took time out from the housework and studying to visit the barn. She especially wanted to see the new colt. It wobbled up on its stick legs when she entered the box stall.

Greta, the yearling colt, whinnied and nudged Virginia for a bit of maple sugar. Virginia had forgotten to bring sugar. My, it had been long since she had been here in the barn!

She stopped, in surprise, to exclaim over the kittens that ran in front of her in the stable. "When were they born?" she asked.

"You haven't been here since the kittens

were born?" asked Papa. "My, that *is* a long time! They were born—let's see—the day after Christmas!"

After Virginia returned to the house, Mama cried. Virginia asked what was wrong, and Mama said, "Oh, Tiny. I just don't have any milk for him, and I can't feed him as well as you do. It makes me so sad. He's just hanging on.

"Every day, I expect him to die, but he's such a tough little fellow. Whoever heard of a spoon-fed baby at his age? But he takes milk from the spoon just like older babies take cooked gruel."

Virginia had a sudden thought. "Mama, could we feed him oat porridge? Please, Mama, let me try. I'd make it very thin, just a little ground oats to add more to his food. Papa says oats is the best feed for the horses, so maybe it will be good for a baby, too. Please, Mama."

"Whatever you think."

Virginia eagerly set out to make the smoothest and softest oat porridge ever. Then she fed him a little bit with the spoon. He ate it without protest. That was the way he ate everything these days, never crying, just eating and sleeping as though he had no right to anything, while the other two babies became more demanding day by day.

Danny came into the kitchen. "What are you feeding him?" he asked.

"A little ground oats cooked with his milk," Virginia replied.

"I hope it works."

Virginia had noticed that Danny seldom helped feed Tiny anymore, except for the two night feedings. Now she asked, "Danny, why don't you help with Tiny?"

"Oh, what's the use?" Danny sounded dejected. "He's going to die anyway."

"He is not!" Virginia screamed at him. Then she realized she was screaming, but she couldn't stop. "He is not going to die. I won't let him. I won't!"

"Well, you'd better find a goat, then." Danny's voice was gruff and harsh.

Virginia was about to give a sharp answer. But suddenly she caught a fleeting expression on Danny's face. Her face softened. She said, "I know you really care, don't you, Danny?"

Her brother ducked his head to hide his eyes. Then Virginia was sure she was right.

16

Jealousy

Virginia woke with a start. It was the middle of the night, and Tiny was crying. What was wrong with him?

Sometimes Tiny whimpered, but this was the first time he really cried. She could tell his voice from that of the other babies because he sounded weak. Yet this crying was urgent.

Virginia went to him quickly. He was chewing on his fist and crying. He stopped to chew, then cried again. Sarah appeared at her side. Tiny must have wakened her too.

"I think it's working," said Sarah.

"What's working?" asked Virginia.

"Tiny's food. See how he seems to be hungrier? I think he's getting strong enough to cry now."

Strong enough to cry now! Virginia hadn't thought of that. Maybe he really was getting stronger. This was certainly the first time he had ever chewed his fists.

Just then Mama came in the kitchen.

"Mama, do you think Tiny could be getting stronger? He's strong enough to chew on his fists and fuss. For three days now, I've been feeding him oat porridge with milk."

Mama came and bent over Tiny. She picked him up. Virginia looked at her eagerly, waiting for her mother's reply.

"Well, it could be," Mama said. She patted him gently. Virginia had a strange feeling deep inside. It was as though Tiny belonged to her and not to Mama.

Mama hadn't held Tiny much before. Why did she notice him now? Virginia felt terribly mixed up. She desperately wanted Mama to love Tiny. At the same time, she wanted her not to love Tiny.

I've taken care of him for so long. Tiny is my responsibility. Tiny is my baby!

She left her mother holding him and heated the milk porridge for the baby.

Then her mother put Tiny down. She turned away from him. There were tears on her cheeks, and she went back to the bedroom without another word.

Virginia fed Tiny, then climbed back into the old love seat that had become her bed in the kitchen. She lay awake a long time, sorting out her feelings.

Finally she decided, *I'm jealous of Mama. Mama hasn't even taken care of Tiny, but he is her baby. No matter how much good care I give him, he'll never be mine. But I won't let that make any difference.*

Someday, Tiny will know I took care of him. Someday he'll be somebody. He might even be president. Papa would think that was being high and mighty — being president. But Tiny may be anyway. Or he might be a world-famous doctor. Who knows what he may be?

17

Sledding

Virginia's birthday came in late January on a day that was perfect for sledding. It had been snowing, but it stopped. The sun shone on the snow and glittered off the icy crust.

Papa came into the kitchen and said, "Mama, could you take care of the babies for a little? It's Virginia's birthday, and I think Virginia needs a break."

When Mama nodded, Papa urged, "Come on, Virginia, get dressed for the outdoors. We're going to the hill with the toboggan."

Soon the four of them, Papa, Danny, Sarah, and Virginia, were flying down the hill together. For two wonderful hours, Virginia forgot all about Tiny.

With Papa guiding the toboggan, they came down the hill again and again. Flying toward the barn, Papa turned the toboggan just in time to coast to a stop by the corncrib. Then there was

a long climb to the top before they could streak down again.

When they came in at last, Mama had hot chocolate ready for them. For a little while, it seemed that the past days had been a bad dream.

Then the babies began crying, all three at once. Virginia rushed around to fix Tiny's milk while Mama fed Laban and Lucy. Papa and Danny went to the barn to do the evening milking. Sarah was busy feeding Babette, who still slept in a box by the stove.

Sometimes Virginia thought that Babette needed as much care as Tiny. Sarah did a good job of taking care of her, though.

Sarah talked to Babette like Virginia talked to Tiny. Babette had quickly learned to gulp up milk from a bucket when Sarah put her fingers in the milk for Babette to suck.

That evening, Papa said, "I still want to find a milk goat."

He sat at the table after supper, looking sad. Now that Tiny was crying like a normal baby, even Papa could see that he might live. If they could just find goat's milk, as the minister had said, maybe he would grow faster.

"Don't the Malcolms have goats?" asked Danny.

"Mrs. Daniels has a goat," Sarah said.

"I've asked the Malcolms and I've asked Mrs. Daniels. They both have goats, but none they are milking now."

"Could we try Ba-ba's milk?" asked Virginia.

"Ba-ba's milk? Sheep's milk is rich, but we could water it down. . . ." Papa was thoughtful. Everyone sat still around the table, thinking. Why not? Maybe Ba-ba's milk would suit the baby!

"Oh, Papa! Let's try it!" said Virginia. "It can't hurt Tiny, can it? We'll give him just a little with the cow's milk. Then each time we'll add a little more sheep's milk until he has only sheep's milk. Maybe he'll do better on it!"

They all agreed to try it. The next morning, Papa brought in the precious milk. "Ba-ba doesn't have much extra milk. Babette drinks most of it, but I think there will be a little extra. Sarah, put a little cow's milk in Babette's bucket so there will be enough sheep's milk to share some with Tiny."

Virginia mixed a little sheep's milk with some cow's milk. Then she boiled it. It was enough for two small feedings after she had added the bit of oat flour to it. Then, after cooling it, she spoon-fed it to the baby. He ate greedily. Now he always ate as though he were hungry. He cried more, too.

Soon Ba-ba's milk was a regular part of his feeding. The baby seemed to thrive on it.

When Babette was big enough to go back to the barn, Sara moped for a day. Then she began going with Papa to the barn to see Babette.

18

Rushing Feet

February drew to a close with a big snowstorm. The wind whipped and howled around the house.

The three babies could no longer be kept in front of the fire on pillows. Papa made a wooden box that held all three, cuddled close together.

Tiny didn't look as small as he had. He was not as big as the other babies, but he was catching up. Virginia worried that the babies would get too cold if the fire got low in the night. So she stayed in the kitchen all night.

Mama and Papa slept in their bedroom together. Danny began sleeping upstairs in his old room. Virginia still slept on the stuffed love seat in the kitchen. She liked to study her spelling into the night by lantern light. Sarah slept on the woodbox. She didn't want to sleep alone upstairs.

One evening, Mama said to her, "Virginia, I think it's time that I take over the care of the babies. Tonight, you go upstairs and sleep in your own bed. That will be so nice for you. You haven't had a night of rest in weeks."

"But, Mama! Who will fix the fire? Who will listen for the babies to cry?" asked Virginia.

"I will," promised Mama.

"All three of them?" asked Virginia.

"Yes," her mother said.

That was hard for Virginia to do, but she went to bed in her own room upstairs. Almost at once, she went to sleep. She was too tired to stay awake, more tired than she had realized.

When she awoke, there was the sound of rushing feet downstairs. She sensed that it was nearly morning. What was happening? The babies were crying, but she could only hear two of them.

Just then Mama came to the stair door. "Virginia, come help me!" came her urgent whisper.

Sarah sat up in bed. "Me, too?" she asked.

"No, I don't need you," Mama said.

Sarah lay down and went back to sleep.

"What's wrong, Mama?" asked Virginia on the way downstairs.

"The babies slept too well. They didn't wake me. When they finally cried, Tiny had come unwrapped. He's been out in the cold, and he's blue. I wrapped him again, but he isn't crying or responding.

"I should never have sent you upstairs to sleep. You took such good care of him. Now, see what I've done!"

Virginia went straight over to Tiny. She picked him up in her arms, turned him on his stomach, and began stroking him as she had done so many nights before. Mama took the other two babies into the bedroom to nurse them. At last the kitchen was quiet.

Holding Tiny on one arm as she had learned to do, Virginia warmed his food, talked to him, and bounced him softly, all at the same time. By the time his food was warm, his lips were no longer blue, and he swallowed his food.

The fire in the stove was reaching a warm glow. Soon the kitchen was as warm as Grandma Katie's house. Virginia held Tiny a long time after she could have put him down. She was thinking of Great-Grandma's words, "Keep the faith and milk the cow!" Now Virginia gave that saying a twist and repeated, *"Keep the faith and feed the baby! Keep the faith and feed the baby!"*

She had fed Tiny so many times when feeding him had seemed useless. But she had kept on anyway. A tiny spark of faith, of believing he would live, had kept her feeding him. And now Tiny would live. She was sure of it.

19

The Bee

It was March. A weak winter sun went down in a purple haze. Virginia saw it because she was on her way to the school with Papa and Sarah in the carriage. There was no longer enough snow for sleighing, but the horses wore their bells anyhow. They made a jingling music as they trotted along.

Virginia was on her way to the spelling bee. Grandpa Daniel had brought Grandma Katie to help Mama with the babies. Danny was home to help, too.

They arrived at the schoolyard just in time to see young Anthony Spears drive up in a handsome carriage with two horses. Virginia felt her cheeks grow warm at the thought of Anthony. She had liked Anthony since first grade, but he didn't notice her.

She entered the school and sat with the other contestants in the front. By the time the bee began, she had twisted her handkerchief into a warm, wet ball. Then it was time to stand up.

Virginia felt herself falling apart. With great effort, she forced herself to think only of the words being spelled. Soon she began to relax. At last, she felt calm and focused. Her confidence began to build.

She didn't even get flustered when she saw Anthony watching her intently. Virginia lifted her head and smiled. She was prepared.

As the words became more difficult, spellers began to drop out. Finally, there were only two of them standing: Melanie Allen and Virginia. Melanie received the word *luscious*. She spelled, "L-u-s-h-i-o-u-s."

The word passed on to Virginia. She paused a long time. At last, she spelled, "L-u-s-c-i-o-u-s." When she spelled *nutritious* a few moments later, the crowd began cheering. Virginia had won the spelling bee. A warm glow seemed to cover everything and everybody.

Melanie spoiled Virginia's pleasure, though. With a peeved voice, she said, "It's not fair for you to stay home and practice all day."

Virginia was speechless. So Melanie thought she practiced all day! If Melanie only knew the hours of baby care Virginia had put in every day! Virginia knew she would have had more time to practice if the babies had never been born and she had been in school.

People crowded around her with their congratulations. At last, the crowd thinned. Virginia stepped out into a cool spring night. There was Anthony, waiting for her. He said, "Congratulations! You were great!" Then he ended with a rush, "May I take you home?"

Virginia thought she hadn't heard right. "What did you say?" she asked.

Anthony's face flushed. "May I take you home?"

Virginia felt herself singing inside. But Papa would never let her. She knew he wouldn't. "I'll have to ask Papa."

She turned to her father, who was talking to a neighbor. At last, she was able to speak to him alone.

Her father pulled his beard thoughtfully. Then he said, "Virginia, you've been doing a woman's job for a long time now. And now you've just turned fourteen. If you want to go, go. I'll be right behind you anyway."

Anthony gave her a hand into his carriage. As they rode along under a full moon, Virginia found herself telling Anthony all about the three babies and her struggle to keep Louis alive. Anthony was a good listener. He asked questions that made it easy to talk.

When they drew up to the yard gate, Anthony asked, "May I ask you again, sometime?"

"Oh, yes!" Virginia said, hoping she didn't sound too eager.

He walked her to the door. Inside, she could

hear Louis crying.

"I have to go. I hear Tiny fussing," she said.

"I like you a lot. Good-night!" Anthony said. He squeezed her hand. Quickly, she stepped inside.

She hummed as she took Louis from Grandma Katie. He quieted immediately. Rocking him, her mind was full of thoughts of Anthony and school. She hummed and sang a happy tune.

20

Secrets

The middle of March came quickly. One day, the weather broke and the sun shone warm. A balmy breeze blew outside.

By now, Tiny was plump and wiggly. He squirmed and stretched constantly.

One morning, Papa said, "Mama, I think the time has come." He winked at her across the table.

"I agree! I think so, too," agreed Mama.

After breakfast, Papa went off on the horse.

"Where is Papa going?" asked Virginia.

"Wait and see!" said Mama. "Now, you and Sarah take the babies upstairs and take care of them. Keep them in your room where the sun shines in the window, so they won't get cold."

All day, the girls stayed in the room upstairs, reading and talking and playing with the babies. All day, they heard secret rushing around downstairs. Virginia thought she heard

Grandma Katie's voice once, but she couldn't be sure.

Danny had been sent to the barn to clean manure from the cow stables. It was a job he disliked, but Papa said it was time to do it, with the weather so springlike.

Now and then Mama took time out to come upstairs and nurse the babies or check on them to see that they were warm and dry. When it was time to feed Tiny, Mama went downstairs and fixed his food, then brought it up for Virginia to feed to him.

About five o'clock, Mama came upstairs.

"Mama, you're all dressed up!" said Virginia.

Mama had on her royal blue dress, so velvety and rich in color that Virginia longed to touch it. Mama's eyes were shining, and she looked like a lady in a picture. Her cheeks even had a hint of color. She was slimmer than she had been in a long time.

On top of her head, Mama's thick blonde braids wrapped around like a crown. Virginia admired her, and her heart began to feel light.

Mama said, "Now, you girls dress nicely. I'll take Laban and Lucy, and you bring Tiny, Virginia. When you've changed your clothes, Sarah, you come down. Virginia, wait till we call you."

Sarah quickly changed her clothes, eager to find out what was happening. She dressed in her best light-green dress, the one that showed off her blonde hair. After all, Mama hadn't said

what to wear. Then she zipped downstairs, pig-tails flying out behind.

What is happening? Virginia wondered. *Why must I wait until last? What could make Mama dress up like that?*

As Virginia changed her clothes, she tried to imagine why they were getting dressed in the evening. She heard Danny come upstairs, heard the sounds of him pouring water into the basin and washing in the next room. Then Danny went downstairs, and it was quiet. Waiting seemed to take forever.

At last, they called her. She picked up Tiny and took the small baby downstairs with her.

She entered the kitchen. There was a shout, "Surprise!" Virginia stood there, stunned. The table was set with the company dishes. Down the middle was a row of candles. There were fragrant pine boughs on the table.

At each table setting was an apple. Virginia, Danny, and Sarah had bowls of candy at their places. Danny and Sarah were standing behind their chairs. Grandma Katie and Grandpa Daniel were there, too. Even Great-Grandma! They all waited for Virginia.

"Here, Virginia," said Papa, motioning her to the one empty place. "Virginia, this is our Christmas. I'm sorry it took so long to get here. Mama and I decided that we still needed Christmas. And it's a very special Christmas.

"Because of you, Virginia, we have three babies this Christmas. We all know that Louis wouldn't be alive if it wasn't for you. So this Christmas is special. It's in your honor. And in the honor of the Christ child."

"But I didn't do anything much," Virginia protested.

"You kept the faith and fed the baby," said Grandma Katie.

"Grandma, you always say, 'Keep the faith and milk the cow,' " said Sarah.

"No, that's what *I* say," said Great-Grandma.

"Well, did you just now make up 'Keep the faith and feed the baby?' " asked Sarah, turning back to Grandma Katie.

"Of course!" said Grandma.

"I made up 'Keep the faith and milk the cow,' too! Many years ago, in Germany," said Great-Grandma.

"What do they mean, anyway?" asked Sarah.

Virginia didn't hear the answer. She was thinking of all the times she was sure Tiny would die, and yet she fed him anyway.

She remembered nights when she was so sleepy her fingers moved from the bowl to his little face without thought. She had fed him over and over and over, with only a tiny spark of hope that he might live.

Tiny was sleeping now. She put him in the bed by the fire, then returned to the table.

Mama asked, "Shall we give it now or later?"

"Now!" said Danny and Sarah together.

Grandma Katie went into the next room. She returned with something made of deep-red velvety fabric over her arm. Standing before Virginia, she unfolded it.

"For you, Virginia," she said.

Virginia's eyes grew big. *A dress!* A red velvety dress for her!

Grandma held it out. Virginia took it. She stroked it and put it up to her cheek. At last, she was able to say, "Thank you."

"Now, let's pray," said Papa. He bowed his head and prayed, "Lord, we thank you especially for our Virginia, who wouldn't give up and who wouldn't let Tiny die. Bless her today. And we thank you for the Lord Jesus who came to earth on Christmas Day just as these three babies came. Amen."

"Now Papa will whistle, 'Away in a Manger,' " said Virginia, happily. "Then we will sing."

"Whistle!" Papa was surprised.

"Yes," said Virginia firmly. "And whistle the last part at least five times. You whistled the last part at least a hundred and five times on the way to Grandma's place."

Papa laughed. "I guess that's not too much to do for *my girl*."

It had been a long time since Papa had called Virginia "my girl." Now, she glowed with delight.

Papa began to whistle. It was the best whistling ever, with trills and vibrato. When it was over, they sang,

The stars in the bright sky
looked down where he lay,
the little Lord Jesus
asleep on the hay.

In the silence that followed the singing, Tiny let out a loud, long "Wah-ah-wah," a half yawn, then went back to sleep. They all laughed together.

In the candlelight, the mashed potatoes tasted wonderful.

Notes

This fictional but true-to-life story, *Virginia and the Tiny One*, took place in the late 1850s. Life was different then. Parents did not tell others that they were going to have a baby. They kept it secret as long as possible. One-fourth of the babies died before reaching a year in age. When a woman was about to have a baby, she wondered whether it would live or die.

Children were not told that their mother was expecting a baby, perhaps to protect them if the baby died. That way a child did not become excited about a new brother or sister and then have to hear that it had died. Often children did not know their mother was expecting a baby because a woman's clothes were bulky, hiding her shape.

Mothers did not go to the hospital to have babies. Most of them never saw a doctor. A midwife came to help the mother give birth. Older children were usually sent to the home of grandparents or neighbors.

Most mothers nursed their babies as well as they could. Bottle-feeding of babies was rare, although baby feeders and bottles were available for hundreds of years. Rubber was just becoming common, so leather was likely still used for nipples. Since Virginia's family was in the mountains, they did not have baby bottles as we do today. Instead, they had to invent ways to feed little Louis.

They tried to feed cow's milk to Tiny, but that often does not suit a baby. A mother's milk has more sugar and less fat than cow's milk. Goat's milk is more like mother's milk. Sheep's milk is higher in total solids (fat and protein) than cow's milk or goat's milk and is easily digested. Mixed with water, it might suit a baby.

You may say "Yuck!" about drinking sheep's milk. Yet you have probably eaten it in lasagna, blue cheese from France, feta cheese from Greece, and Romano and Ricotta cheeses from Italy. Sheep's milk is also used for yogurt, ice cream, and drinking. Baba's milk had to be used carefully because sheep give only a little milk. One good cow can give as much milk in a day as a sheep gives in a month.

Older people tell stories about using whiskey as medicine. The alcohol in whiskey is a drug. Whiskey was used to wash out wounds and to kill germs and the pain of dentistry or surgery. Now we have other medicines, solutions to kill germs, and painkillers.

For Christmas, the children in this book received candy. The German immigrants did not give many gifts, if any, for Christmas. This is why it was unusual and meaningful for Virginia to enjoy the dress as an extra gift.

For some families, there were few gifts until the 1900s and even the 1950s. Many descendants of such families, living today, can remember Christmases without gifts.

The Author

Esther Bender, M.Ed., is a writer and former teacher, living near Grantsville, Maryland. She taught in public schools for twenty-three years.

Since 1984, Bender has published more than a hundred short stories and articles for adults, and stories for children. She is a member of the Society of Children's Book Writers and Illustrators.

A 1974 graduate of Frostburg (Maryland) State University, she received departmental honors in early childhood education. In 1981, she earned a master's degree in elementary education with certification as a reading specialist.

At FSU, Bender studied reading under Dr. Judith Thelen, a past president of the International Reading Association and a wide-ranging speaker. Since graduation, she has taken courses in children's literature and writing fiction and books for children.

Esther is a daughter of Alton and Rhoda Miller, Springs, Pennsylvania. She attended

Springs Mennonite Church and became a member there. After high school, she moved to the Washington, D.C., area, where she attended Hyattsville Mennonite Church.

In 1976, Esther discovered she had Parkinson's disease. When she was unable to function as a "normal" person, she was on her "own personal ocean in the middle of a storm." Eventually she was blessed with new medicines to control her disease, computer technology to open a new world of writing and publishing, and a devoted marriage partner.

Today Esther and Jason Bender live quietly and happily in a cedar house in the woods. They both are readers and computer "addicts."

Esther Bender's short stories for children have been published in periodicals such as *Clubhouse, On the Line, Primary Treasure, Our Little Friend, Action, Happiness,* and *Story Friends.* Stories and articles for adults have appeared in local newspapers, in *Christian Living, Purpose, United Parkinson's Foundation Newsletter,* and other publications.

Bender has written for and edited *The Casselman Chronicle,* published by the Casselman Valley Historical Society. She has prepared publicity for the National Pike Festival and contributed to the *National Pike Travel Magazine.*

Virginia and the Tiny One is Bender's sixth book published by Herald Press (see page 2).